Treasure of Short Stories

ANANTINEE (JHUMPA) MISHRA

Invincible Publishers

First published in India in 2018

ISBN: 978-93-87328-97-6

Invincible Publishers

G-120, Sushant Lok III, Sector 57, Gurgaon-122002

Registered Address: Opposite Kasturba Ashram, Radaur, Haryana - 135133

Printed at Thomson Press (India) LTD

Acknowledgement

Writing an acknowledgement is a way of expressing thankful feelings and gratitude to people of great magical feelings. So, first of all, I thank the Almighty for showering me with the strength to clear all the hurdles in my way to accomplish my first ever piece of writing. I then take the opportunity to thank my Gods in human form, my beloved parents, my MAMA for letting me try my limits and my BABA for helping me through them. I then thank my grandfather for his continuous efforts in making me understand my abilities, and my grandmother for all those helpful and understanding words of inexpressible comfort. I also wish to mention my most caring Amma, who gave me immense comfort at times when I was worried and overwhelming strength when I felt weak. I would also take the moment to express my heartfelt gratitude to all my honorable and knowledgeable teachers, very supporting and encouraging family members and loving friends for all their good wishes.

Love,

A

Contents

Preface

The book '***Treasure of Short Stories***' is a collection of tales which evoke certain deep feelings through intentional and expressible writing. The stories consist of various and exceptional morals which can help one become a better person. You will meet and learn ignorance and tolerance from Satrupa, the young girl in *Supposed to be Friends,* who is bullied because of her talents, while in *The Sapphire Ring,* you will find superstitious nonsense taking over logic. As you help Vikas, the easily anxious boy, complete his homework in *Vikas's Homework Dilemma*, you'll see Kushal, the stubborn boy, justifying himself in *Stubborn Kushal*. *Anshulika's Realisation* sees Anshulika as a lazy liar, though she changes, while *Therapy of Kindness* witnesses the change in Shekhar because of a kind dove and a repaying sparrow. It is very selfless to be kind, but it is all the more so when you are not supposed to be doing so, which is shown in *Kathleen Faces Her Own Daring* by a young girl Kathleen. *The Golden Bag* records Ameksha's adventures as she loses everything in a terrible earthquake, but gets a chance of winning it all back with the help of an ordinary golden bag, while Ashima faces torture by Alisha in the face of love in *Jealousy and Problems*. *A Fun Trip* sees three best friends Kanchi, Kamya and Shruti together on a trip where they enjoy each other's company and the scenic beauty of Khandala. *Will and Won't* oversees the forcing of thoughts in a true sense by a mother upon her daughter, Nishtha. *Minku Realises His Mistake* is a story of humour. *Kindness Revealed* is the story of Gabrielle, a greedy girl and the elder sister of Isabelle and Clarabelle, while *Shardha Regrets Bullying* is the story of Shardha, a bossy girl who regrets her attitude.

Wish you an enjoyable reading!

Supposed To Be Friends

You must have heard the famous quote, 'A friend in need is a friend indeed.' You must also know the meaning of this quote, that is–a friend who is there for you when you need him or her is a true and loyal friend. This story shows the struggles of Satrupa to find loyal and trustworthy friends.

Satrupa was an intelligent and beautiful girl, studying in class fifth in the city of Delhi. Her well behaved personality and intelligence caused a stir of jealousy among her fellow classmates. But she had the precious friendship of her four best friends–Anita, Maanyata, Kirti and Abhay. She was particularly teased for her friendship with Abhay, as he was a boy, and Satrupa's classmates jeered that Abhay was her puppet boyfriend. But Satrupa couldn't care any less. One day, as soon as she entered her classroom, whispers started. Some people even pointed at her. Satrupa could not understand what had happened. Little did she know that the day was going to be very chaotic and dramatic because of some stupid rumour. Suddenly, as if appearing out of thin air, Abhay pulled her aside and said, 'Listen to me, Satrupa. That Maanyata is not your best friend. In fact by the look of it, she might be your worst foe. You confided in her your secrets which she has now leaked to people who are jealous of your success. Together, they have devised a whole new thing out of it. They are telling people that you topped the second semester exams by cheating. They are even spreading the rumour that you had leaked the final mathematics paper. Maanyata is not your friend, Satrupa, and those girls, Antasia and Aveha, are always up to something or the other to discredit you. C'mon, let's go to our class teacher Malaya ma'am and complain to her about Antasia, Maanyata and Aveha. Anita and Kirti are waiting for us in the corridor. They too feel completely disgusted and are convinced about Maanyata's doings. C'mon!'

Grabbing Satrupa by her wrist, he turned to go, when Satrupa stopped him and said, 'Don't speak rubbish, Abhay. Maanyata will never do this. I know and am convinced about Antasia and Aveha being bullying girls, but I am sure that you must have heard wrongly about Maanyata. There is a possibility that to cover up their misdeeds, Antasia and Aveha labeled Maanyata as the culprit. This would give them two benefits; first, there will be whispers and rumours about me and all the blame will go to Maanyata, and second, they will take my strength and separate Maanyata from me. Remember, they are always trying to break our–I mean, yours, mine, Kirti, Maanyata and Anita's–unity and friendship. I am not saying that you are wrong. You care about me, that's why you are putting blame on Maanyata without even thinking, I am not saying that you don't trust Maanyata, but Abhay, please think about it with a cool mind. I am sure that you will understand. Anyhow, we will wait till Malaya ma'am comes to the class. Then we will talk to her regarding Antasia and Aveha. Sometimes, the truth is hidden behind a dense fog of misunderstandings, but that doesn't mean that the fog can't be cleared. It can be cleared by the emotions of trust, friendship and unity. You guys are my courage and strength to stand up to Antasia and Aveha's misdeeds. If you start fighting with one another, how am I supposed to deal with them? Look, Malaya ma'am has arrived. Let's go grab a seat for both of us in the front so that it will be easier to talk to her. I don't want Antasia and Aveha fluttering near us, trying to manipulate ma'am that I am a bad, arrogant and attention seeking girl.'

Quickly moving and dodging awkward stares, Abhay and Satrupa found a bench right in front of the teacher's desk.

Tringgg! sounded the bell, indicating that the class teacher's period had begun. Malaya ma'am took out her register to take the attendance, but before she could start reading the names aloud, Satrupa told her all about the rumours, whispers and finger pointing that was taking place in the class. She also told ma'am about the likeliness of the fact that all of this is was being done by Antasia and Aveha, but also made her promise that she wouldn't tell anyone that she doubted them. Malaya ma'am consoled Satrupa by saying that she should forget about this matter and that she would talk to Antasia and Aveha directly. As for the rumours and whispers, she assured her that they would subside in a few days, so she only had to endure them for a day or two. By noon, it became clear that Malaya ma'am had talked to Antasia and Aveha very strongly and sternly, as they shot glaring looks at Satrupa, Anita, Kirti and Abhay, which made all of them intently gleeful and jubilant.

Their second last class at 1:15 PM was Library. The seating arrangement was pinned to the library notice board. Kriti and Anita, with three of their classmates–Aditiya, Shivani and Shruti, were arranged on table 4, while Satrupa, Abhay,

Maanyata, Antasia and Aveha were arranged to sit at table 6. Though she had taken Maanyata's side that morning conversation, Satrupa was not entirely convinced of Maanyata's innocence herself. Her friend had lately been spending a lot of time with Antasia and Aveha with her head bent down as though planning something very important and exclusive with them. Satrupa didn't know what to believe and what not to, but that library period cleared that her doubts about Maanyata were perfectly true.

Satrupa was on her way to the fantasy shelf to get her favourite book, Harry Potter and the Half Blood Prince by Joanne Kathleen Rowling (popularly known as J.K. Rowling), when she heard whispers about herself, 'I think we should steal silly Satrupa's books. With the terminal periodic tests coming up, she will die of agony.'

'Whatever we do, we should make sure that she suffers from such terrible and unbearable pain that she will always regret complaining to ma'am about us. I know she did that.'

'Guys, I think we should make one of our prized possessions disappear and put the blame on Satrupa. I will take my mom's jewel, make a copy of it and when everybody is downstairs for

P.T., I will hide it in Satrupa's bag. The rest you know... Then you both can tell ma'am that you saw Satrupa steal the jewel. A can bet a 100 rupees that my master plan has inspired awe in both of you.' The voice had a bit of smirk in it.

The other two voices agreed.

Satrupa recognised each and every voice well. The first voice belonged to someone who had hated Satrupa since the first day of nursery... Aveha Kullad.

The second voice belonged to someone who had always cursed Satrupa, sometimes under her breath while sometimes on her face...Antasia Singh.

But the third voice surprised her most of all. It belonged to someone who Satrupa had always thought a friend, but had really been a foe; someone who always showed love to her face, but had hatred fo her deep down; someone who had broken the trust of Satrupa Raichand into a million parts...Maanyata Khan.

Maanyata made Satrupa's insides squirm. She felt traumatized. Many questions were racing in her mind, Why had Maanyata done this? Had Antasia and Aveha manipulated her? But even if they did, why didn't Maanyata come to her? Had it been that Maanyata did come and she, Satrupa, did not listen? Had Abhay, Satrupa, Anita and Kirti shunned Maanyata out? Had that resulted in their separation? Answers to all these questions could only be achieved upon a direct confrontation with Maanyata.

'Oi!' said Abhay, snapping his fingers in front of Satrupa. Kirti and Anita were standing by him. She didn't even realize where her feet had carried her. 'The bell rang minutes ago. Why are you looking so anxious? I swear, you are getting more absent minded day by day. Blimey! I forgot, it is the maths period now. Let's go, else we will be in serious trouble.'

Abhay turned to go, when Anita grabbed his wrist to stop him from going. He was about to retort, but she silenced him with a look. Steadily looking at Satrupa, she asked her what was going on. Without another hint, Satrupa burst into the full story about the voices of Aveha, Antasia and Maanyata that she had recognised, the questions in her mind and her thoughts of confronting Maanyata about all of this. The further she went with her story, the more pronounced their grimaces became. When she had finished with her story, everyone gave her the same advise: ignore it. They all soothed her by saying that she, Satrupa, was a mature girl and this was too small matter for a confrontation, as she should not give a dirty minded girl like Maanyata such importance and value. They all told her that she should rather care for everything that was good in her life like their friendship. From that day, Satrupa ignored Maanyata and her life became more honest and liveable.

The Sapphire Ring

On the much awaited night of Christmas, everyone in a small village in Washington D.C. was celebrating. Well, almost everyone. One man had a very dull and depressing atmosphere in his life and house. He had various troubles going on in his life. The man's wife had just expired on the twenty fifth of December. He was so heart-broken that he shut himself inside his bedroom on the day of his wife's funeral. The brothers of the man took the coffin of the man's wife to the nearby graveyard. As they all were very tired, they quickly dug a grave for the coffin, then went back to their respective homes after consoling the man's children and wishing them luck.

At the stroke of midnight, the graveyard was completely lonely and empty. The graveyard's security guard had just finished his duty and was waiting for his substitute to arrive and take over the watch. Suddenly, he remembered that the woman (the man's wife) who had been buried that evening was wearing a very prestigious Sapphire ring, but it had not been removed from her hand after the last rituals. He decided to dig the coffin out and keep the ring for himself as he was very poor.

With a torch and a knife, he entered the graveyard. Slowly, with small but heavy footsteps, he moved towards the woman's tomb. Now, he was beginning to get frightened. His hands were starting to shake with fright. He calmed himself down by thinking of all the money that he would get after selling off the Sapphire encrusted ring inside the tomb. He was also feeling very uneasy, as he knew what he was doing was wrong. He felt torn between the emotions whirling inside his mind. Somehow, as if by a miracle, he found the courage to go all the way to the woman's tomb. He prayed to the Almighty all the way. After praying heartily, he took out his torch from the waist pocket of his double breasted jacket and started digging the tomb of the woman to retrieve the prestigious and expensive Sapphire ring. Very slowly, he started to dig out the coffin. His hands were shaking completely now. The white marbled coffin of the woman slowly came to view underneath the bouquets of white and red roses. Over the smooth marble were engraved the words:

Here lies the noble Mrs. Margaret Ketchikan. We pay her our last wishes and may she rest in peace.

'Sorry, Mrs. Ketchikan. I have to feed my family. I hope you understand my compulsion and need for money…' muttered the security guard to himself as he opened the coffin with trembling hands. When he saw the woman's face, he felt quite shocked. He had half expected the woman to look ragged and rotting, but she looked quite beautiful and charming instead. She had rosy red lips, pink cheeks, sweeping eyelashes, a fair face and jet black hair.

'What a beauty! She is so charming,' muttered the security guard to himself. He plucked out a white rose from one the various bouquets that had been lying atop Mrs. Ketchikan white marble tomb, and placed it over her dead body. Then, he looked at her fingers where the Sapphire encrusted ring sat glittering. Very slowly, he stretched his fingers over to the woman's hand. He seized her fingers and started to pull her ring out. But no matter how hard he tried, he could not wrestle the ring out. It seemed as if the lady had warped it with some magical force. He was left with no other choice. He pulled out the knife from his jacket pocket and quickly cut off the woman's ring finger.

No sooner had he done that, the woman's hair rose up. Slowly, she sat up and began to pull herself out of her grave. Paralyzed with fear, the security guard felt goosebumps rising on his neck line.

"S-spare-e mm-me pp-ple-ease-e,' he managed to stutter. The woman, not paying any heed to him, turned the other way and started walking out of the graveyard, taking long strides. The security guard had meanwhile lost his consciousness out of fear.

At last, the woman arrived at the destination that she had longed to come to–the house of her husband. Looking around, she found a stone and hurled it at one of the windows of the house.

It went straight through the dining hall to the bedroom of the man. It crashed against the bedroom door and fell down with a thud. Hearing the commotion, the feeble body of the frail old man was stirred. Slowly, he got up and went over to his bedroom door to unbolt it. He half wished to stay in his bedroom, but he had to stop (whom he thought it was) the thief from taking away the precious and sweet memories of his beautiful and charming wife. He stumbled across the dining hall towards the main entrance of the house.

He opened the door and shouted, 'LOOK! WHAT DO YOU THINK YOU ARE DO–oh!' He now saw the face of the woman clearly. 'You ar-are a gh-ghost o-of my ww-wife, aren't yo-you?' he muttered.

'No, I am not. I had not died when your family members buried me. I was alive, I sensed everything, but could not cry out for help. But today, I sensed immense pain when the security guard cut off my finger to take off my prestigious Sapphire encrusted ring, and my senses returned. I came to meet you as soon as I could. Please believe me, please do. You can even touch me if you don't believe me,' croaked the woman pleadingly.

Very swiftly and daringly, he held out his hand to touch the soft and silken skin of the woman. She was real. He realized that when he touched her. Not waiting for another moment, he embraced her. Soon, they realized that they should thank the security guard with the Sapphire ring, for if he hadn't been there, the woman would probably be buried still. They went back to the graveyard where the shaken security guard was just regaining his consciousness. They told him the whole story and thanked him with the Sapphire ring. The ring had turned out to be a lucky one for the Ketchikans. As for it, we don't know where it went afterwards. So, now you know what superstitions do–remove the logical ability and brilliance of our extraordinary minds. Never believe in these brain-washing and manipulating things.

Vikas's Homework Dilemma

Vikas Mehta was a twelve year old boy studying in a private school in New Delhi. He was an athletic boy. Though he was also good academically, he absolutely dreaded Mythology. He did not have any specific reason to say why he did, it was just that he didn't like the subject.

One afternoon, when he returned from school, his was very anxious. When his mum opened the door for him, she immediately came to know that something was wrong. Vikas was lost in his own world. He was biting his nails, which always meant that he was anxious. 'What happened, Vikas? Is there something wrong?' his mum asked, ruffling his hair.

'Yes, mum. Today, we have been told to read three passages and answer questions based on them as homework for Mythology. Those passages are incredibly long and I didn't understand a word of them. How am I supposed to answer the questions? On top of that, our Mythology teacher has told us that he will be taking our notebooks for correction tomorrow, so I have to complete the homework today itself. I am already feeling very tensed,' replied Vikas.

'You scared me, Vikas. I can help you with your work. You can take help of the internet as well.

You get anxious too often and over silly things. Okay, don't make a face now and come inside. I have made your favourite *pav bhaji* for lunch. You can take *dahi lassi* with it,' said Vikas's mother with a tinkling laugh. Reassured finally, Vikas went inside to enjoy his afternoon.

After eating his stomach full of *pav bhaji*, Vikas lied down to take a short and power nap. Seconds later, or so it seemed to Vikas, he was shaken awake by his mother. 'I am sorry, Vikas, but I won't be able to help you with your homework. Your dad's colleague has invited me and your dad for a movie and dinner. We cannot say no. We are leaving in another fifteen minutes. But I do have a solution to your problem. I just called your best friend Meera's mum. She told me that you are always welcome at their house, so you can complete your homework there with Meera and her mum's help. It might get very late by the time we come home, so you can have dinner at their place as well. You can come back home by 9:30 PM. Are you ready to spend your evening at Meera's place?' she asked in a hurried manner.

'That is a superb idea, mum. But how am I supposed to get there?' replied Vikas in an excited voice.

'Your father and I will drop you off at her place on our way to the restaurant. Her father can then drop you back home. Hurry up and change into your trouser now. Grab all your homework books and come to the hall. Be quick,' replied Vikas's mother.

Vikas did as he was told and ten minutes later, he was in the hall. He listened to his mother while she told him to behave himself at Meera's place. She was repeatedly saying, 'Remember to chew without opening your mouth. Don't call Meera's mum, auntie. Call her Mrs.–what is her last name–yes, call her Mrs. Singh formally. And behave-'

'I know, mom! If it is done, can we go now? It's getting late and I doubt if all your mannerisms are going to make a better impression if I turn up late,' Vikas finally bellowed, losing his patience and peace of mind.

After a fifteen minute's drive, Vikas found himself ringing Meera's doorbell. Mrs. Singh greeted him with a clinging hug and said in a cheery voice, 'Meera is waiting for you in her room, Vikas. I will get you some sandwiches while you both complete your homework. And don't hesitate to ask me or Meera if you want something else. Go on, enjoy your evening.' Vikas muttered a word of thanks and proceeded towards his best friend Meera's bedroom. He entered her room and was transfixed. Meera had decorated her room very lavishly. There was a high bed with a pink coloured quilt on it. Right behind the bed, painted on the wall was a picture of Meera from when she was around six years old. On one side of the room, there was a very long window with velvet curtains over it. Next to it was a bookshelf which carried Meera's favourite books from the fantasy genre. There was Chronicles of Narnia and Harry Potter along with other famous sets of fantasy novels. There was also a small snacks table in front of the window, with circular chairs for sitting around it. On the extreme left was a recliner where Meera loved to sit and read books. The floor was covered in a velvet carpet.

'Vicky!' shouted Meera as soon as she saw him. *Vicky* was the nickname given to Vikas by Meera, since she thought that the name Vikas was very boring.

'Very good to see you, Mer. You will have to help me with our Mythology homework today,' Vikas said in a delighted manner.

Meera frowned and replied, 'I will, but you have to stop calling me Mer. It annoys me very much.

My proper name is Meera Tanvi Singh. You can call me MTS for short, if you like.'

'Why don't you call me VM for short, then? My proper name is Vikas Mehta. Your *Vicky* drives me crazy. If you start calling me VM, I won't call you Mer anymore,' Vikas replied.

Meera thought for a moment, then said, 'That is never going to happen. So you can keep calling me Mer.' Vikas stared at her for a moment, then both of them burst out laughing.

The evening passed by merrily. Mr. and Mrs. Singh were very affectionate people. They urged Vikas to take triple helpings of everything that was served for dinner that evening. Meera helped Vikas with all the homework, and when he asked her where she got all that knowledge from, she simply said *books*. While being driven back home by Mr. Singh, Vikas told him how he had become very anxious regarding their Mythology homework. Mr. Singh laughed and said, 'My dear boy, this is life. You should not waste your childhood worrying about small things such as this. Enjoy your childhood. It comes only once in your life.'

Stubborn Kushal

I ♥
DELHI

This story is based on a true incident that took place in the city of Delhi. Though it is a vast city, once you get connected to it, you cannot part from it, no matter what. This story is about a boy, named Kushal who got attached to Delhi, but had to leave it. But, you know, if you are truly attached to something or someone with your heart and mind, a magical link is created in that connection. That bond becomes immortal without any fantasy filled turn. Even if the Almighty wants then, that bond can't break. Let's read on to know more about Kushal's attachment and feelings towards Delhi and whether he leaves it or not.

'Yes?' said the receptionist in an irritated voice upon answering the landline call. Whoever had called had just interrupted an important document counting that the receptionist had been doing. 'Good morning, madam. This is Mrs. Tanushree Kapoor this side. I am the mother of Kushal Kapoor who studies in class seventh A. I have called because of an urgent matter. I want to withdraw Kushal from his school because of...err...a situation which cannot be avoided,' said the voice, now registered as Mrs. Kapoor, on the other side.

'But ma'am, we can't let you take Mr. Kapoor without you giving us a detailed and satisfactory reason for such a withdrawal. I suggest that you come to school and write a leave application for him. If the reason is found worthy enough, the Principal will sign it. It would only take half an hour then,' said the receptionist in an exasperated tone.

'I certainly understand the school rules, but this is a tight situation, madam,' said Mrs. Kapoor. After a short pause, she continued, 'Okay, alright. I am reaching the school in half an hour. You keep the leave application ready.'

'Okay, thank you very much, ma'am. I shall keep the leave application ready by the time you arrive, and a very good day to you,' saying so, the receptionist hung up.

Twenty minutes later, a taxi pulled up in front of Yama Hoshi International School and a woman in her thirties stepped out, looking very apprehensive. She paid the taxi fare, straightened her dress and started climbing the marble staircase that led to the main entrance gate of the school. The woman, Tanushree, was exceptionally beautiful. She had wavy brown hair which lay untied and reached down to her waist. Her eyes were very bright with brown pupils, while her lips had a pinkish glow. She was tall and slender, and was wearing a blue dress made out of delicate silk with gold embroidery around her neckline.

Stepping inside the main building, she headed for the desk which had a plate reading 'RECEPTION'. 'Good afternoon, madam. I am Mrs. Tanushree Kapoor. I must have an appointment regarding a leave application signing,' said Tanushree upon arriving at the reception desk.

'Yes, Mrs. Kapoor. Your appointment is fixed. I am giving you the leave application form. Please fill it appropriately and hand it back to me. It shall take it to the attendance office for inspection, and if the reason is found satisfactory, it shall go to the Principal for his signature,' replied the receptionist, swiftly handing her the application form along with a pen.

'Will it take much time? I mean, I am in a hurry to pick Kushal up,' said Tanushree anxiously.

'It will take the required amount of time, ma'am. I request you to please make yourself comfortable on the sofa after giving me your form. Please cooperate with us, ma'am,' said the receptionist, pointing to the visitors' lounge in front of the desk.

'Oh. Okay. Alright, I will do so. Thanks for the help,' replied Tanushree, pink in the cheeks.

Ten minutes later, Tanushree returned to the desk and handed back the application form to the receptionist, saying, 'Here is the application form.'

The receptionist asked Tanushree to wait at the sofa, and took a sweeping look at the form. It said-

NAME OF PARENT WITHDRAWING WARD: Tanushree Kapoor

NAME OF STUDENT: Kushal Kapoor

REASON FOR WITHDRAWING STUDENT BEFORE SCHOOL HOURS: Transfer formalities. Kushal's father, Viraj Kapoor, has got transferred to Canada. The flight is tomorrow morning, so Kushal and I have to go to the studio right away to complete the photographical formalities. The household work has to be completed too.

IF THE ABOVE ANSWERS ARE INSPECTED AND PASSED BY THE OFFICE OF ATTENDANCE, IT SHALL GO TO THE SCHOOL'S PRINCIPAL FOR SIGNATURE. IF IT IS NOT PASSED, THEN YOUR WARD WILL NOT BE PERMITTED TO LEAVE BEFORE THE SCHOOL HOURS OFFICIALLY END.
Yama Hoshi International School, Delhi.

The receptionist shook her head and moved towards the Office of Attendance. Half an hour later, when Tanushree was twisting her fingers in anxiety, a clerk came from the Office of Attendance and handed a piece of paper to the receptionist. She stole a glance of the paper and called out, 'Mrs. Tanushree Kapoor, your application has been passed. It has been signed by our Principal too. I shall send a clerk upstairs to fetch Mr. Kushal Kapoor.'

Tanushree let out a sigh of relief and said, 'Oh, that's great. Please call Kushal quickly so that we can leave. Thanks.' The receptionist now turned towards the clerk and instructed him to get Kushal from class seventh A. Five minutes later, Kushal hurried down the stairs with his bag over his shoulders. Reaching Tanushree, he asked, 'What happened-'

'I will tell you on the way back home. Come on,' said Tanushree, interrupting Kushal's question. She took his bag from his shoulders and placed it over hers.

'Have you fetched Kavya from her school?' Kushal asked about his younger sister who studied in class fifth in another school.

'I told you, we will talk on the way back home,' snarled Tanushree, hushing Kushal up. They exited from the school building and hired an auto rickshaw from the main road. 'Now listen, Kushal. Your father has been transferred to Canada over an urgent matter. We have to pack up most of our stuff and shift it there by plane. Kavya is at home already, sorting out the stuff that she wants to take or leave. Once you reach home, you better do the same,' Tanushree said in a hurried voice.

'Mom, I cannot and will not leave Delhi. It is my home and I don't care about anything else. You, dad and Kavya can go to Canada. I will live at my best friend Vikrant's place,' whispered Kushal in a frantic voice.

'Kushal, don't you understand? This would be-' started Tanushree, but Kushal cut her off, saying, 'No, I don't understand, mom. In fact, you don't understand. I have got all my friends–Vikrant, Saurav and Sonali here. My memories remain here in Delhi, and you want me to leave all of it and go with you to some stupid foreign place!' Kushal pointed to his mom in dire accusation.

The auto rickshaw driver turned around and stared at the pair of them. Kushal did not regard this, but Tanushree waved her hand airily and hushed him up. She had always been very touchy of what others thought of them. 'Kushal, control yourself and your anger. I don't like the way the driver is staring at us. Let us get back home and talk more freely,' she whispered in Kushal's ear. Kushal opened his mouth to retort, but stopped. Ten minutes later, the auto rickshaw pulled up in front of a house with blue walls. It had a handsome plate reading, 'THE KAPOORS'.

'Yes, yes, this place. What amount should I pay?' asked Tanushree, as soon as the rickshaw stopped in front of their house. Kushal jumped out of the rickshaw and rushed towards home. Tanushree, having paid the fare quickly, rushed after Kushal. As she reached him, she saw that he was ringing the doorbell ferociously. The door opened and a girl of about eleven years came out. Unlike her parents and brother, all of whom had jet black hair, Kavya Kapoor had curly brown hair which fell down to her waist. Her perfect almond shaped eyes were a delicate shade of brown, same as her mother's. She was smiling serenely at her brother with her soft pink lips, but alas! Kushal didn't smile back.

'Out of the way, Kavya. You would at least have the brains to do so,' he snapped at her, pushing her flat against the door. Kavya looked half scared and half angry, but did not make any retort. She spared one intimidating look for her mother who entered behind Kushal. Together, they went in the direction that Kushal had stormed off.

'So!' started Kushal as soon as he saw his mother and sister entering the hall. 'You both, along with dad, took the big decision to shift to Canada, and didn't even bother to care for my opinion. No listen, Kavya, don't interrupt. Tell me, am I not a part of the Kapoor family? If I am, then-'

Kushal's monologue was interrupted by his mother, whose voice was unnaturally high. 'How dare you, Kushal Kapoor? Don't you understand that you and Kavya are not mature enough to take decisions on your own yet? Your father and I have taken a decision that we know will have a good effect on the whole-'

She was interrupted by Kushal again, 'What about my benefits? You-' He was interrupted again, but by his father this time who came bursting through the door just then.

'Tanushree, I talked with my boss and my transfer has been cancelled. I am so happy that I invited him for dinner. Can you believe it? He said ye-' He stopped abruptly when he noticed the expressions on each of his family member's face. Before he knew what he was doing, Kushal threw himself into his father's arms and sobbed on his shoulder. 'Oh, dad! You scared me half to death. How could you possibly think for even a moment that I would leave Delhi?'

His father patted him on the shoulder gently and asked what he had said to Tanushree and Kavya. He told him everything, after which Viraj (Kushal and Kavya's father) made him understand that deep affection for something was good, but one had to act with patience and maturity if a problem arose, and that a reasoned discussion could solve any problem, be it big or small. Kushal understood his father's words and apologised to his mother and sister. They lived happily forever.

Anshulika's Realisation

Drishika Sankar and Anshulika Sankar were cousins who lived in the same neighborhood. Both of them were extremely good friends, though very different individually. While Drishika had perfectly round brown eyes, Anshulika had, pale eyes. While Drishika loved to read books and perform gymnastics, and was thus perfectly slender, Anshulika preferred to laze around in her house. Drishika had an elder sister, Chitra (Chitralekha Sankar), so she had learned to share all her things since childhood. Anshulika, being a single child, had always been subject to a biased treatment. At school, Drishika preferred to settle arguments and quarrels with a reasoned discussion, unlike Anshulika who liked to abuse rather than discuss.

One Friday morning, when Drishika was in her room getting ready for school, Anshulika came bursting in. She had a pen in one hand and a piece of paper in another. She was already ready and had an anxious expression on her face.

'Drish! Have you completed the Geography homework essay based on Latitudes and Longitudes that we received yesterday?' she asked hurriedly.

'Yeah, I have. Why?' asked Drishika.

'Thank God. I was unable to do it yesterday. Give me your essay so that I can quickly write mine down too,' replied Anshulika with a sigh of relief.

'You know I disapprove of copying, Anshu. Still, you are saying so. How will you learn if you copy? By the way, why did you not complete the homework? It was quite easy, so you wouldn't have needed auntie's help either,' said Drishika with a stern expression on her face.

'Come on, Drish. If you let me copy, I will write the essay here. When I write, the things will automatically go inside my head. What is the difference, weather I write it from the book or from your essay?' replied Anshulika impatiently.

'May I repeat, why did you not complete the homework yesterday itself?' asked Drishika, folding her hands across her chest.

'I had a very bad headache yesterday,' said Anshulika promptly. But that was a lie. She had been watching T.V. and chatting with her friends all evening the previous day. Though Drishika knew that she was lying, she nodded and reached out for her bag to take out her essay. Within the next fifteen minutes, Anshulika had completed the homework and Drishika had also got dressed, so they both had a piece of toast and some hot chocolate quickly at Drishika's place and left for school.

Their school was a fifteen minute's walking distance away from their home, so they walked the route, discussing the periods that they had that day. '....and I will complete my Civics homework during the break because it is the last period at 1:15,' Anshulika was saying. On reaching the school, Anshulika hurried away to sit with her friends, while Drishika went to sit with her SBF (School Best Friend, as the term goes), Karishma Kaalin.

'Hi! I tried calling you yesterday, but you didn't pick up your phone,' said Karishma as soon as Drishika came to sit beside her. Before Drishika could reply, another smirking voice interrupted their conversation.

'Maybe, Drishika Sankar's family doesn't earn enough to pay the landline bills. Or that's another matter that they can't even afford one.' Naisha Sharma swept by, a maddening and mocking smile plastered on her face.

'It is not your family that we are talking about, NN,' came another voice. Drishika realised that it was Anshulika who had spoken. Though she was a lazy liar, if one abused someone whom she was close to, it might be the last thing one ever did.

'Shut up, you faithful sidekick of Dirty Drishika. And what is NN?' snapped Naisha with an air of superiority.

'Nauseated Naisha,' said Anshulika, howling with laughter. Everyone around them who was listening (that is, the whole classroom) laughed, including Drishika and Karishma, as both of them disapproved of abusing. Her face furious, Naisha swept back to her seat along with her two faithful accomplices.

'You should not have picked a fight with Naisha, Anshulika. She shall try to harm you and make your school life miserable for calling her Nauseated Naisha,' said Karishma with concern, addressing Anshulika.

'Don't worry, Karishma. If she does, she will become a magnet for trouble,' replied Anshulika smiling.

'Good morning, class.' Their class teacher entered the classroom and wished the class.

Karishma, Anshulika, Drishika, Anshulika's friends and everybody else who was taking part in their conversation went back to their respective seat and chorused back, 'Good morning, Deepika ma'am.'

'Settle down, settle down,' said Deepika ma'am, waving a careless hand while taking the attendance register out from her handbag. Deepika ma'am taught the class English, Mathematics and Civics. 'Now class, I want to make an announcement before I start with the attendance. We have our Civics class in the seventh period today, but I swapped my period with your Hindi period. That means, your Hindi class will take place in the seventh period, while my Civics class shall take place in the second period. Let me remind you, I shall inspect your homework then,' said Deepika ma'am straightening up.

Drishika half glanced at Anshulika. She was looking anxious. Drishika knew why. Anshulika had thought that since the Civics period was after the break, she would complete the homework during the break. Wrenching her thoughts away from Anshulika and her homework, Drishika tried to concentrate on what Deepika ma'am was saying.

The periods before the break passed without any great incident, unless you count Anshulika being scolded and made to do sit-ups in Civics for not having completed her homework. The break passed by quite well too. Anshulika, Karishma, Drishika, Chitra (Drishika's elder sister ate lunch with them), Meenakshi and Lekha (Anshulika's friends) ate their food together, joking and gossiping. Then came their fifth period: Geography.

As Kamal sir came into the class looking grim and serious, everybody's breath intensified. Kamal Kukreja sir was a very strict, aggressive and grim Geography teacher. He quelled everyone by just giving a stern look with his piercing eyes. 'Before I start my class, I want each and every person in this classroom to come to my desk and submit their homework essay on Latitudes and Longitudes, or suffer my displeasure,' Kamal sir said in his deep voice, frightening everyone. 'Who will like to come first?' he continued, looking at everybody.

'I will come first, sir.' The whole class turned around to see Anshulika who had spoken, her hand raised in the air. Kamal sir peered at her suspiciously, then nodded grimly. Anshulika got up gracefully, took out the essay from her desk and advanced towards his desk. She handed out her essay and turned back to return to her seat, when Kamal sir said, 'Wait. Stand here.'

Anshulika was taken aback, but followed all the same. The further Kamal sir read Anshulika's essay (practically, Drishika's), the more wide his eyes became. Finally, he asked, 'You wrote this?'

'Yes, sir.'

'All by yourself, without anyone's help?'

'Um...obviously, sir.'

'Really unexpected, Miss Sankar. You are finally working hard. Well-Well. Full marks.'

Anshulika seemed as though her birthday had come early. She muttered thanks and collected her essay from him. She was about to leave when she stopped, took a deep breath and said, 'Sir, this is not of my own writing. My cousin, Drishika Sankar, had written this. I copied it from her this morning.'

Kamal sir looked at her and then to everyone's surprise, he smiled and said, 'I knew this is not your writing. I fully know the way in which Miss Drishika writes. I just wanted to see weather you would come out with the truth or not. How come you said it?'

'Sir, I realised the power of hard work and determination when you said, 'Full marks.' And this is Drishika's hard work. I cannot take credit for it,' said Anshulika, thoroughly surprised.

'And for that, it is full marks,' said Kamal sir. Anshulika beamed at him and walked back to her seat. She had finally learned the importance of truth and hard work.

Therapy of Kindness

This story revolves around a small boy who realizes the importance of kindness, gratitude and politeness through the lively story of a dove and a sparrow narrated to him by his mother.

Shekhar was a talented boy brimming with energy, studying in the Bourneville School for secondary boys. He was a curious listener and an obedient student in the classroom, while being a mature sportsperson out on the field. Alas! Not everyone possesses all the qualities evenly. Shekhar was an awfully rude and arrogant boy. He would often boast about his huge collection of medals and trophies won in various athletic tournaments or subject related quizzes all the time to anyone who would listen. Gradually, his friends started staying away from him, both at home and at school. This only increased his sense of superiority. One day, after returning home from school, Shekhar told his mother that one of his classmates, Taneeveeksha, had received scolding earlier that day for doing the sums given in the Mathematics homework wrongly. 'Why should I care if she is some dumb old crackpot?' continued Shekhar after repeating the story smugly.

'Shekhar, don't talk about your friend-'

'SHE IS NOT MY FRIEND!' bellowed Shekhar, interrupting his mother. While being arrogant and rude, Shekhar was also awfully short-tempered.

'Shekhar, if not a friend, she still is your classmate. Please respect that. Let me tell you a story about a dove and a sparrow. Listen carefully-

'Once upon a time, there was a kind and gentle dove. She liked to help other animals and birds, even if it costed her her own life. One rainy morning, the kind dove was enjoying a piece of fruit cake in her nest while watching the raindrops splatter through the branches. Suddenly, she heard a cry. She looked sideways to find a sparrow caught in a bird trap, probably set up by a hunter. Not worrying about he own safety, the dove flew towards the trap and started to tug the sparrow out of the giant bird trap. No matter how hard she tried, she could not free the poor sparrow from it. Moreover, the rain was now pounding hard, making visibility close to zero and her claws slippery. Suddenly, she had an idea. She quickly found a marble with a sharp edge-'

'How does it always happen that the main character finds the required stuff at exactly the right moment?' interrupted Shekhar irritably.

'Shekhar, the text of the story is not important, but the lesson or learning that it gives us, surely is. Never judge anything by its outer presentation, always look for the inner thoughts. So, listen carefully,' his mother replied with a hint of annoyance in her voice.

'She quickly found a marble with a sharp edge in a nearby bush and started to cut the ropes that had entwined the trap tightly around the poor little sparrow. At last, the rope broke into two pieces. The sparrow was injured a little, but was quickly hoisted around the neck by the kind dove and was immediately flown to the dove's nest. There, it was given a set of warm blankets, and some coffee and grains.

'Thank you so much! If you had not been there, who knows what might have happened. I might have been dead by now. Please tell me if I can do something for you. It will be an honour and a pleasure,' said the sparrow gratefully.

'Oh, come on now. We can do all these sappy talks later, sweetheart. For now, it's time for some gossip,' replied the dove mischievously. Though the sparrow pretended to forget, she remembered that she had some kind liabilities to pay off.

Several weeks passed after the rainy incident. The dove had forgotten that several weeks before, an incident had occurred where she had saved the life of an innocent sparrow. She had just returned from her daily grain and worm hunt that day. She was siting in front of her nest on a branch, eating her meal, unaware that a hunter had his arrow aimed up at her feathery white neck. The hunter was already having dreams of a sumptuous dinner comprising of roasted dove meat with wine and salad. Suddenly, a large brown feathery ball appeared in front of him, thus distracting him, which resulted in the arrow slipping from his hands and hitting the bark of the tree with a loud THUD! Alarmed by the sound, the dove looked down to see her sparrow friend distracting the hunter, and quickly rushed inside her nest to hide. The hunter, now a little scared, started to scatter away from the place as soon as possible.

The sparrow flew upwards towards the dove's nest and stepped inside. As soon as she laid down her first step, she thought there was another attack. The dove came flying to her and hugged her tightly.

'How can I ever thank you enough for-for…you know what,' started the dove and started sobbing hysterically.

'By making me a strong cup of tea,' said the sparrow sweetly. The sparrow consoled the dove with her kind words.

Shekhar's mother stopped at this point in the story. 'I hope that I don't have to continue any further,' she said, putting emphasis on the last few words. 'Any boy with an average sensitivity of an adequate human must have been touched by just this much. I think you do have the ability, Shekhar.'

'I am indeed very touched, mum. Today, you've taught me to be happy for others and to dance in their happiness, while consoling them and mourning in there sadness. Thank you, mum, for teaching me the principles and the meaning of life,' replied Shekhar, now on the verge of tears.

'If I have indeed taught you so many things, I need a fee for it. Will you help your classmate Taneeveeksha overcome her fear of mathematics and become better at it. Will you, Shekhar? Will you do that for me?' asked his mother hopefully, shaking him a bit.

'That goes without saying, mum. In fact, I think I will make her some notes so that it becomes easy for her.' Excited by his own idea, he got started with his work. That was perhaps the start of a fruitful friendship between Taneeveeksha and Shekhar.

Kathleen Faces Her Own Daring

This story, or rather this incident, takes place in the heart of London, in Christopher Square. Here lives Kathleen Qutora, a twelve year old who enjoys a peaceful and very normal life with her loving and pampering parents. Let's read and discover how a lonely road in Christopher Square challenges Kathleen's daring, fearlessness and kind attitude.

Kathleen Qutora was excited. That very day, in her Christ Sq. Primary Department School (C.S.P.D.S.), she was told by her teachers that she had been selected for an inter-school competition which was to be held at Cassandra Williams Senior Educatory School the following Thursday (eight days from that day). It was an ultimate story writing competition. She and her best friend, Williosa Abercrombie, were now walking down the empty and shuddering lane, discussing Kathleen's chances of winning the competition.

'Well, I suppose that as it is an on-the-spot competition, my chances of winning are seventy percent. If it had been a write and bring one, my chances would have been a hundred and ten percent. I am quite sure of that,' said Kathleen, slyly but practically. Suddenly, she caught sight of the boundary wall, reading that someone named

Nairna Singh was missing. But her eyes were not focused on the photo of Nairna Singh, but on an injured bird rolling down the wall. Even though she could not understand bird language or sign language (at any rate), she immediately came to realize that the injured bird was in a lot of pain and agony. It was clear from this distance that it had now started to whimper in pain (as far as Kathleen could assume).

Without thinking what she was doing, Kathleen ran towards the injured bird and kneeling down beside her. She kept it in her lap, thinking hard about how she could save the innocent bird from nasty circumstances. 'Oi! What are you doing, Kath? Your mum hates stains and even those nasty pesky things. And of course, she is right. Those dirty things make our hands filthy, Kath. And that one is also rolling in the mud. Eww!' said Williosa smugly and perhaps a bit as though she was terrified, which she was.

'Oh really, Willi? Since when have you become so cold hearted to ask such harsh questions? Since when, Willi, since when? You call them filthy, do you, Willi? But then, what are your thoughts? Go away Willi. Sorry, Williosa Abercrombie. Get out of my sight!' shouted Kathleen across the road.

'Fine! I will go, but then don't come to me when your mum slaps you or punishes you because of your stupidity and silliness. You will regret your words and doings some time later, you will!' saying so, she pulled her bag over her shoulders and marched off in the other direction. Kathleen had heard her, but did not reply. She had more important things going on in her mind than Williosa's misgivings.

She quickly rummaged through her bag and found a blue handkerchief with a white flowery margin. Taking the bird in her hands, she wrapped the handkerchief around it and kept it down to zip up her bag's chain. To her horror, she saw that her hands were covered in something red. It, of course, looked horribly like blood. She was now feeling scared. Brushing away the negative thoughts that came to her mind, she closed her bag's chain and reached towards the injured and perhaps even unconscious now. Racing her brain over what to do, she bolted upright. A brilliant idea had just occurred to her and she wanted to execute it right away.

She remembered that her mom had gone out to her aunt's house and wouldn't return till 4 PM. She stood up and carrying the injured and unconscious bird in her arms, set out towards her house. As soon as she reached her house, she kept the bird on the lawn bench and took out the duplicate pair of house keys from her purse which was kept inside her bag. Quickly unbolting the door, she carried the little bird inside. Her home was a spacious one. It had three bedrooms, on pantry, one kitchen, one terrace, one lawn and two bathrooms. Keeping the bird on the coffee table, she hurriedly got the first aid kit and sat on the squashy armchair beside the coffee table. Unwrapping the napkin (which was now covered in blood), she took out the rolling bandages and started wrapping it around the poor bird's wing which was injured and now covered in dark reddish blood. Carefully squaring the bandages, she put the contents back in the first aid kit and went to put it back in the pantry drawers.

While returning, she went to their kitchen and poured out some milk in a bowl and some single grains in another. Carrying the tray carefully, she stepped out of the kitchen, but stopped dead in the hall. Her mother was standing there, her arms folded and a frown on her face. 'What is all this, Kathleen? What is this bird doing here? Why is there blood on your frock and on the lawn bench?' asked Kathleen's mother. She was not shouting, but her voice was stern.

'M-mom I-I–' stammered Kathleen, but her mum interrupted.

'If you have not done anything wrong, then say it confidently and fearlessly. The one who says nothing but the truth is always right.'

Gaining confidence, Kathleen repeated the whole story. When she had finished, her mother said, 'And you expect me to scold you? I love you even more now. I am proud of the way you didn't loose your head and never feared my reaction. I am so proud of you.' Saying so, she hugged her.

Then, what happened? I think you might already have guessed...competition practice. You remember, right?

The Golden Bag

It was a joyous day. It was Ameksha Kumari's wedding. Everyone was in a hustle. The ladies had settled themselves in the spa and makeup room. All of them were discussing the various aspects of their looks, their traditional dresses and of course, Ameksha's luck

Ameksha's father was a rich merchant of silk. His one and only daughter, Ameksha, was both his weakness and strength. His money or empire never worried him, but his daughter's mild innocence did. Ameksha, while being very rich and beautiful, was also extremely kind. She promised anyone anything without giving it a second thought. But again, luck always favored Ameksha. Her fiancé Akash Malhothra had been Ameksha's best friend since childhood. Like his father-in-law, he was also a very rich man. He was an architect. A few weeks back, he had proposed to her on a trip to Kullu Manalli which they had taken together to discover their fears. Everyone agreed that Ameksha and Akash were a perfect couple.

Meanwhile in her dressing room, Ameksha was pacing up and down. Half an hour back, her mother had told her that she was going to give her a priceless gift which she had to take care of all her life.

'What if I am not able to take care of it? I am not terribly careful about my possessions. If it is an ancient family heirloom, then–oh!' Ameksha was muttering to herself when she saw her rigid and stiff looking mother entering her dressing room, tightly clutching a golden bag.

'My dear,' started Ameksha's mother. 'My dear, this golden bag contains a very prized treasure belonging to you father and me. It contains some fruits. No...listen, Ameksha!' she said as Ameksha showed signs of interruption. 'You may not understand this treasure right now, but I am sure you will when it is the right time. But right now, do I have your word that you will take the utmost care of it? Your word that you will make its protection your first priority? Do I have your word? Do I?' continued Ameksha's mother.

'Of course, you do have my word, but perhaps if you could just tell-?' replied Ameksha with a hint of annoyance in her voice.

'I don't blame you for your curiosity, dear, but your father and I know that this treasure will always be an immense relief to you in your troubled times. Please have faith in us. Now, the guests will be arriving shortly, so I shall take leave. I will send in your friends shortly to help you get ready,' replied her mother, her voice decreasing to a whisper with every word she said. Saying so, she handed the golden bag cautiously to Ameksha. Ameksha didn't reply, but merely nodded.

The wedding rituals proceeded as normal; *Varmaala, phere, bidaai* – in short, everything that a wedding must ensure. After all the rituals, even the wind seemed to be celebrating and rejoicing at the faithful union of the two souls. But soon, a very strong wind started blowing, uprooting trees and making the house roofs shake. Though many tried to stop them, Akash insisted that he and Ameksha should go to Delhi straightaway (a three hour's drive from Ameksha's father's villa), since they both had their tickets for London the following morning. Akash had an architecture contract there and could not afford to lose out on such a globally important deal.

They set off in their car with a couple of security guards for protection. Their route included a very dense forest where it was very dangerous and risky to travel at night. But still, under those nasty circumstances, they had to take the route as it was the only significant one which bypassed to Delhi. As they entered the forest, Ameksha felt a shiver of fear. The trees looked like old daredevils looking greedily over them as they passed under them. 'There is nothing to worry about in this forest. Some idiots have started this nonsense superstitious rumor that this forest is haunted and dangerous,' started Akash consolingly on seeing Ameksha's fearful face. 'Nothing will happen to you because you are with me,' he added mockingly.

'I know. But still, I feel...I can't express it in words. I hope you understand my plight,' replied Ameksha, gripping Akash's hand fiercely in hers. Suddenly, the driver said, 'Sir, ma'am, the car has broken down. I can repair it, but if you get down for just a few minutes, it will make the work easier. Sorry for the inconvenience, madam,' he added to Ameksha apologetically.

'It's nothing, really,' said Akash, waving a hand airily, but Ameksha didn't say anything, nor did she show any gesture or sign of agreement. While they were waiting, someone tugged at Ameksha's *ghaagra*. She turned around to see a girl, about sixteen years of age, looking up to her and crying. She was wearing bridal clothes too, though they were all ragged, dirty and even torn at some places. She also wore a mangalsutra and two short earrings.

'Didi, please help me. My husband and in-laws are nowhere to be found. I am feeling very hungry, but I have no food to eat or any money to buy it. Please help me. Believe me, I am not conning you or lying to you. Please,' said the girl tearfully. Hearing this, Ameksha knelt down and had just started to unscrew her earring to give to the little girl, when suddenly, the girl stopped her and said, 'Didi, I don't need your jewellery or money, but if you could just give me something to eat and help me find my husband and in-laws.'

Ameksha didn't know what to do. She didn't have any food to give to the little girl. Suddenly, she remembered with a jolt–the golden bag. She also remembered that her mother had told her to keep it safely all her life and to make it's protection her utmost priority, but it only contained some fruits, she thought.

This poor girl is asking so pleadingly that I can't refuse her food. Anyway, even if mum even comes to know, I don't think she will be angry because whatever I am doing is for a good cause. This will make this girl happy and I will feel better after doing something good too. Thinking so, she brushed away the negative thoughts and decided to help the girl. 'Didi,' said the girl, shaking her back to her senses.

'My dear girl, what is your name? How come you are here in this forest? Anyway, don't worry. My husband Akash and I will surely help you,' said Ameksha, trying to cheer the girl up.

'My name is Shwadha, didi. My husband, my in-laws and I were crossing this forest to go to our village on the other side, when suddenly, I turned back and found them gone. I searched from them and called out their names, but nobody answered me back. Thank you so much for your kindness. I will always remember you,' said Shwadha, fresh tears brimming over her eyes. But this time, the tears were of happiness and gratitude.

Suddenly, Ameksha's driver appeared out of nowhere and said, 'Ma'am, the car has been fixed. Sir is already sitting inside. Who is this ragged girl, madam?' His question at the end came as a very irksome one.

'I don't like your tone, driver. Shwadha will accompany us in the car until we find her family members. I want my handbag removed from the luggage cart, so I can give her some food to eat. And I want all of it to be done very quickly,' shot back Ameksha, her voice unusually stern. The driver looked rather shocked, but obeyed the orders all the same. As soon as she got her handbag, she took out her golden bag and was just untying the knot when Shwadha said in a rather timid little voice that the bag had very pretty embroidery and that it looked quite expensive too.

As soon as she had said this, a thought occurred to Ameksha that this bag only contained some fruits, so why not give it to Shwadha. She had also developed a liking for the bag. Thinking so, she handed the bag to Shwadha and said humbly and sweetly, 'My dear, if you like this bag then do take it. It contains some fruits. Eat them and you will feel better. Now, let us go and sit in my car. My husband, our driver and I will help you find your husband and in-laws.'

Shwadha beamed at her and looked happily flustered. Muttering a word of thanks, she followed Ameksha back to her car. 'Where were you? I had started to worry–who is this ragged girl?' asked Akash as soon as they came to view, wrinkling his nose with the last few words.

'This is Shwadha. She is here because…' said Ameksha, recounting the story and her decision, though she said it as if the golden bag had been given to her as a refreshment. She neither mentioned the conversation with her mother in the dressing room before the wedding, nor the promises she had made to her over the safekeeping of the golden bag.

'Oh, okay. Of course, we should help Shwadha then. Good that you gave her some fruits to eat. Our hunger is nothing compared to the girl's. After all, we did have a feast right after our wedding,' said Akash as soon as Ameksha finished her story. 'By the way, I am Akash. You can call me Akash *bhaiya*,' he added, smiling at Shwadha. Shwadha didn't say anything, but returned his smile with a shy grin.

'There! They are my in-laws and that is my husband,' shouted Shwadha after a quarter of a hour of search, pointing jubilantly towards a family of three huddled together, looking scared. 'Oh, I am so happy to see them. Thank you so much, Ameksha didi and Akash bhaiya. Perhaps God sent two life savers to me because of some good deeds that I might have done in the past.' Shwadha jumped out of the car and ran towards them, throwing her arms around her in-laws. They hugged her back, looking equally happy and perhaps a bit surprised. Breaking away, she recounted to them the story of how Ameksha and Akash had helped her find them.

As soon as she stopped talking, Ameksha and Akash witnessed their tears of gratitude, received their thanks for saving their daughter-in-law and dismissed their apologies for having occupied their precious and valuable time. At last, Ameksha and Akash settled down in their car and waved them goodbye, making their way back towards Delhi.

'Feeling good? I always do when I help someone and see them smiling cheerfully,' said Ameksha as soon as the car gathered speed.

'I am also feeling good, but right now my shoes are not. They are pricking my feet,' replied Akash, struggling with his shoes.

'Permettez moi to assister vous,' said Ameksha jokingly in French and bent down to help him.

***

Eleven years passed since that stormy night. A few changes had taken place in the Malhotra family. Ameksha Malhotra was now a mother to an eight year old girl, while following up with the grief of losing her parents and in-laws in a car accident. Akash Malhotra was now the president of the Indian Architectural Board (IAB) and was a successful man. Their daughter, Aarti Janaki Malhotra, was a very sincere, talented, sophisticated and intelligent girl. All was well. What the family didn't know was that a major uproar was going to enter their peaceful lives.

One fine Sunday morning, while Akash and Aarti were inside the Malhotra Manor playing video games, Ameksha went to their backyard lawn to inspect the flowers. Suddenly, the place where the gigantic Malhotra Manor stood started shaking. The windows broke, crashing through the outer walls. A major earthquake was taking place. Inside, Aakash consoled a terrified Aarti by saying, 'It is just a normal earthquake, Aarti. It will perhaps last a minute or two. No need to worry-'

THUD!!!

A brick slid out of the ceiling and hit Aakash straight on the head. Clutching his head, he dropped to his knees, whimpering in pain. A cloud of dust had now erupted inside the manor. Several more bricks came crashing down the hall. Dodging them, Aarti rushed to her father's aid and said, 'Daaad! Are you alright? Please answer–OW!'

Tripping on a wire, she had hit the wooden sofa. Her hand was now bleeding very badly.

'Are you fine, Aarti? I am. Answer me, Aarti!' shouted Aakash.

'I am fine, dad. But how do we get out of this wreckage?' said Aarti, clutching her arm where the blood was the wettest and the darkest.

'I say that we get out of the back door and move through the lawn. Ameksha must be waiting for us there,' shouted Aakash, his voice hoarse due to the dust. He attempted to smile, even though his face was all dirty and covered in dust. He had a deep cut on the forehead and his shirt was torn at the shoulder.

Meanwhile in the backyard, Ameksha was horrified. The walls of the manor which held so many precious memories and relationships, was collapsing in front of her eyes and she was not able to do anything to save it. A gust of wind had blown away with it all the moments which held a special place in Ameksha's heart. Her husband and daughter were trapped inside, perhaps hovering between life and death. Her neighbours had rushed out to save themselves too, but none of their houses was collapsing. Everyone realised that Aakash and

Aarti were stuck inside the manor. Very silently, they came and patted Ameksha on the shoulder, repeating the same lines in pity, 'We are very sorry to hear.'

'MY HUSBAND IS NOT DEAD. THANK YOU VERY MUCH FOR YOUR HELP,' she finally bellowed at a man who had repeatedly been trying to convince her to hold a funeral from his company. She felt angry at all those who believed Aarti and Aakash to be dead. She knew they were alive and could sense their presence, but she too was anxious. Without knowing what she was doing, she ran towards the Delhi border. The Malhotra Manor stood close to Delhi's border with Haryana. She didn't know for how long she ran. When she stopped, breathless, she saw a sign:

WELCOME TO HARYANA.

WE WISH YOU A PLEASANT TIME HERE.

She stood staring at the board for a few moments. Then, without a warning, everything went pitch black.

Ameksha blinked stupidly. Something soft was ruffling her hair. What exactly it was, she didn't know at the moment. She opened her eyes and saw a woman ruffling her hair. She had round eyes, milky blonde skin and pink lips. Her jet black hair fell loose over her shoulders. Ameksha didn't know why, but her face looked oddly familiar.

Seeing that she had woken up, the woman's good natured face broke into a relived smile. 'Thank goodness, you have woken up. Your mind must be bombarded with questions, so let me start from the beginning. You fainted in front of the Haryana sign board and injured your head. Fortunately, my husband was returning from Delhi at the same time and saw you getting hurt. He got you to our home so that we can take care of you. You are on our drawing room sofa right now, as we didn't have the guest room ready when you arrived. You were seriously injured, so I had my entire attention on you. We are a family of five: My husband Atharva, our son Ankit, my mother-in-law Shirsha mom, my father-in-law Avdhut papa and I,' she said in a sweet voice.

'Thank you so much for your generous hospitality. For how many hours was I unconscious?' asked Ameksha in a quivery voice. The lady checked her watch and gasped, 'Good Lord, it is 7 AM already. My mother-in-law must be coming down any moment now. I should get her toast and coffee ready. Excuse me,' and she hurried towards what Ameksha assumed was the kitchen.

Ameksha blended perfectly well with the family. The lady Shwadha and her husband Atharva accepted Ameksha as their own sister. She called Shwadha's in-laws as aunty and uncle, and little Ankit adored Ameksha like his mausi. He reminded Ameksha of her own Aarti. She had not told any of the family members of her past. She did not know why, but she had taken the decision in full consciousness. Though she couldn't understand why, the lady's name, Shwadha, sounded oddly familiar.

There was another thing about the house that made Ameksha curious. It had to do with the prayer room. Shwadha had told her that it contained something very precious that she and Atharva didn't want exposed, so only the two of them were allowed in the prayer room.

Ameksha helped Shwadha in cooking and cleaning, while also helping Ankit with Mathematics and English. She had now become a part of the family. One Sunday morning, Ameksha was playing two sided cricket with Ankit, when the ball went flying in the air and crashed through the prayer room's window, landing inside. Ankit started whining and crying for the ball.

Finally, Ameksha decided to go to the prayer room herself to get the ball for Ankit. As she entered the prayer room, she saw that it had some garlands, incense sticks, idols and a golden bag with embroidery. At once, Ameksha understood everything. She now knew why Shwadha looked and sounded familiar. She shouted with happiness, 'SHWADHA! AUNTY! UNCLE! COME QUICKLY TO THE PRAYER ROOM! HURRY!'

The door banged open and in came Shwadha, her lips pressed thin with fury, followed by aunty and uncle, both looking terrified of Shwadha's anger. Before she could say a word, Ameksha burst into the story that had taken place eleven years ago to prove the evidence. She also told everyone then that the name Shwadha sounded familiar to her because she had met them all eleven years ago. After getting to know each other, Shwadha and Atharva tried to help Ameksha with finding her family, though they couldn't succeed. Aakash and Aarti seemed to have vanished off the face of the Earth after having escaping from the terrible earthquake. It was however the start of a very long friendship.

Jealousy and Problems

Jealousy is one of the most harmful addictions which destroys families and relationships. This addiction was once taken up by the seven year old Alisha, who always held a grudge against her sister Ashima who was both physically and mentally more beautiful than her. Though she ignored and dismissed many incidents which pointed out that Alisha was jealous, she realized the truth at last. What will happen to Alisha and Ashima's relationship? To know, read on...

Ashima was a very happy and carefree girl. She excelled in studies and sports.. Her parents, Akshita and Ashish Mehta, were very rich and perfectly lovely to their only daughter, Ashima. All was well, until a problem came into Ashima's life. Akshita got pregnant again. It was still not a problem with Ashima until Alisha, her younger sister, was born.

Since the day Alisha turned seven (and Ashima turned thirteen), she started hating her elder sister. It was merely because of the love and affection Ashima got for her huge collection of medals and trophies she had won in various competitions held in her school. Alisha started doing all kinds of mischief which she did not know were certainly going to put her into a lot of problems.

One bright Sunday morning, while Ashish and Ashima had gone jogging and Akshita was washing clothes in their laundry house, Alisha sneaked into Ashima's room and broke her most favourite dolls and tore her most beautiful dresses. 'Everyone thinks of me as the excellent Ashima's younger sister, but no! I will make you suffer so much, dear sister, that you will regret prospering so much in studies and sports. If not that, you will certainly wonder why Alisha became your younger sister or rather your worst enemy!' roared Alisha to herself.

She didn't realize that she had crushed the bow pin so tightly that drops of blood had started to appear on its underside. She spilled ink all over the pearl white gown that Ashima was going to wear to the masquerade ball that was going to be held at there school the coming week. Suddenly, she heard Ashima climbing up to the landing of the first floor. She quickly wiped off the blood on the pink curtains of her room.

'Alisha! Want to have break–what has happened? Why is your face so pale and sweaty?' asked Ashima, entering the room.

'Uh! Nothing. I just-just was looking for my pen-stand. Do you have it by any chance?' stammered Alisha.

'Nope. If you want, I can lend you one. I have two.'

Alisha was about to say no, when Akshita called both the girls downstairs for their sandwiches.

***

Sooner or later, Ashima had to find out about the mischiefs of her younger sister. 'ALISHAAA! COME DOWN STRAIGHTAWAY, OR I WILL MAKE YOU!' shouted Ashima at the top of her voice. Alisha came down running. She made a face as if she was an innocent girl whom Ashima was putting behind the bars for no reason.

'What happened, Ashu? Why are you shouting for Lishu like a maniac?' enquired Akshita, quite concerned.

'When you learn about what has happened, it will be even worse. My shouting will then sound like only a whisper to your and dad's ears,' shot back Ashima with a voice choked with emotion.

Alisha ran forward and hugged her mom. 'Mom-mom, what has happened? Why is sis-'

'Don't you dare call me your sister, you wicked witch! I would rather die than be the sister of such a feelingless and insensitive girl like you!'

interrupted Ashima. Unable to control herself any longer, Ashima blasted out her story of how there was ink all over her masquerade gown, how she had found Alisha in her room, looking all pale and sweaty, and of course, the blood stains on her curtains and the bow pin. ‘So, that proves that Alisha is the culprit-’

‘How can you be so sure that I am the culprit? I mean, without any proper evidence or proof, you cannot claim anything!’ shouted Alisha, interrupting Ashima. Angry crocodile tears were sparkling in her eyes.

Ashima let out a roar, ‘Mum and dad might believe you, but I can’t because I know exactly what kind of a person you are! You are an evil, manipulating-’

‘Enough, Ashima! Just because you father and I have given you the liberty, doesn’t mean that you are going to bellow out anything. Hold your tongue, I see that it is sprinting very frequently these days,’ interrupted Akshita, her voice sounding dangerous. Ashima glared at her mom for a few seconds, then looked at her dad for support, but he shook his head too.

‘Fine! Both of you may believe Alisha, but I will not. I see that because of her, this partiality has started. But you will regret your temper with me, mum. The day this girl goes too far, all because of your pampering and ignorance, I will be forced to do something that I am sure you won't like,' said Ashima angrily. Before Akshita could respond to her, she stormed off to her room, her curly brown hair dancing behind her.

Akshita and Ashish stood there, dumbstruck. Feeling that leaving in a melodramatic way would be the best thing to do, Alisha pretended to brush away her crocodile tears and left the room.

Meanwhile in her bedroom, Ashima has collapsed onto her bed and was now muttering angrily to herself, 'She thinks that she will make my life miserable...but I won't let her...' She wished to have someone whom she could hold on to and ask for advice. Suddenly, she had an idea. Why hadn't she thought of it before–Alok, Tapsee and Alishka. They had been her three good friends since nursery. Alishka was her best friend, along with Alok. Tapsee was a close friend, but reliable though. She grabbed her phone from the table beside her bed and texted Alishka -

'Hi, Alishka! Listen, it is an unavoidable emergency. Can you meet me at Sizzling Sakorna's café in about half an hour? If you can, round Alok and Tapsee up too and get them along. See you at Sakorna's.'

Within minutes, she got Alishka's reply -

'Sure, Ashima. Any hint about the 'UNAVOIDABLE EMERGENCY' that you are facing?'

Ashima typed back -

'Thank God, you and the others are coming. I can not handle the problem without you lot. Well, I will tell you the exact problem at Sacorna's café, but the root of the problem is my sister, Alisha. Won't say anything else here. Bye.'

Alishka replied back -

'Alisha? You freaked me out for a moment, Ash(Ashima). Well, I hope it is nothing serious. See you at Sizzling Sacorna's.'

Ashima didn't type a reply, but simply kept her phone back on the table and lay down on her bed once again with nothing but bitter thoughts for company. She thought about Alisha, whose name meant noble. Was her name appropriate for a person like her, she thought, remembering that she had named her sister. She had got the idea from her best friend Alishka's name. She had always believed that Alisha would be a remembrance of her friendship with Alishka. She could not believe that the same Alisha whom she had cradled in her arms, was now plotting against her. Carried away by the train of her thoughts, she didn't notice that twenty minutes had passed since she had promised Alishka to meet at Sizzling Sacrona's along with Alok and Tapsee.

Suddenly, she glanced at the wall clock and saw that it was 2:20 PM already. She jumped, as though she had received an electric shock, grabbed a comb from her dressing table and started combing her long curly brown hair. After that, she wrenched her wardrobe open, seized a red and black frock from it and quickly changed into it. Now grabbing her purse, she quickly stuffed into it a two thousand rupees note which she had just withdrawn from her savings. She made a dash for her phone, shut her bedroom door and descended the stairs.

As she reached the dining hall, she found her mum and dad, along with Alisha, sitting at the dining table and having lunch. 'Big deal! So no one had bothered to check whether she was hungry or not, let alone call for lunch,' thought Ashima bitterly. Just as she turned the door knob of the main entrance of her house, her mother called, 'Control your ego, Ashima. Come and have lunch-'

'I will not have lunch were she will,' replied Ashima, pointing at Alisha. Before any of them could open their mouth, she said, 'I will have lunch at Sizzling Sacrona's with my friends. I will be back by 3:30.' Without waiting for their approval, she wrenched the door open and was out of the house.

Breaking into a run, she didn't stop until she arrived in front of a large door which had a shiny plaque reading, 'Sizzling Sacrona's'. She opened the door and entered. It was a brightly decorated room with pink confetti and wall hangings. 'Over here, Ashima!' bellowed Alishka, waving her hands frantically over her head. Spotting her, Ashima half-walked half-ran towards their table. Seated beside Alishka were Alok and Tapsee, both wearing anxious expressions. Alishka flung her arms around Ashima as she reached her, Tapsee did the same too. Alok gave her an one armed squeeze.

After taking her seat between Alishka and Alok, Ashima said, 'Thank you very much for coming. It means a lot.'

Alishka waved an airy hand and had just started to say, 'Don't be si-' when they were interrupted by the waiter who had come to take their order. They couldn't just sit and gossip at the restaurant after all.

'Two white sauce macaronis, two grilled charcoal chicken burgers, and four fresh lime sodas sweet,' said Ashima without even consulting the menu. She had come here a few times before and knew the menu by heart. The waiter looked enquiringly at the other three, but when they nodded feverishly in agreement, he looked quite abashed and gave Ashima a look before leaving all the same.

'So, what is the problem, Ashima? Alishka told me that it had something to do with you sister–what was her name–ah yes, Alisha,' asked Alok, who had till now been staring at the waiter with a look of incredulity on his face. Ashima then recounted the whole story to her friends.

'Seriously, Ashima? Seriously?' cried out Tapsee when Ashima completed her story.

'This cannot have happened. You loved that girl like anything, Ashima,' Alishka's reacted when she heard the story. Before Alok could react, their lunch arrived and they had to cut their conversation short. After much gulping of the lunch, they decided to talk further at school the next day. After their quick goodbyes, Ashima hurried home in one direction, while Alishka, Alok and Tapsee went in the other direction.

As she opened the door to the living room upon coming home, she found herself facing her mum and dad sitting in the living room. Alisha was standing there too with tears flowing down her cheeks. As soon as Akshita saw her daughter, she got up and flung her arms around her. 'Oh, I am so sorry, Ashima. I should have believed you. I came to know about Alisha's mischievous activities while you were away. She was talking to herself in her room, devising new plans to harass and hurt you, while I listened standing at the door. She also confessed that she was the one who broke the trophy that you had won at the quiz competition a few days back. The maid had seen her, but we refused to believe it and dismissed her from the job. And a few months back, when she stole your diamond necklace and burned it, your father and I thought that you had been careless and scolded you so much. It was all because of her. I am also very sorry for my temper this morning. Please try to forgive me,' said Akshita tearfully.

'Forgive me too, Ashima. I should have backed you and tried to see from your point of view too. I am sorry,' added Ashish guiltily.

'It is alright, both of you. What you did was a mistake, which I am sure you won't repeat. I have forgotten it and you should do the same. Alisha, I also said some very bad and hurtful words to you in the morning. Will you forgive me?' asked Ashima smiling.

'You forgive me, Ashima. I don't know how I got so carried away by the hatred and jealousy for you,' sobbed Alisha.

As soon as Ashima looked into her eyes, she understood that this was no pretend-plea. Alisha was really pleading for forgiveness. 'It is alright. You became jealous because you see only my success and not yours. You are more talented than me, but you overlook that fact. Jealousy is love and hatred at the same time. Because you have committed the crime of jealousy, you shall repent it by dismissing the hatred and keeping only the love,' said Ashima with an assuring smile.

Giving back a watery chuckle, Alisha hugged her tightly. Ashima's family was perfect again. The next day at school, when Ashima told Alishka,

Alok and Tapsee this news, they all said the same thing, 'We told you so!' Ashima just smiled and didn't bother to correct them. Ashima Singh was perfectly happy.

A Fun Trip

This story is set in the vast and modern city of Mumbai. In this city, there lived a twelve year old girl, named Kanchi Agarwal. This story revolves around the beauty of friendship and Khandala through a fun trip that she takes with her friends during her summer vacations.

It was a lazy summer morning. Kanchi was sitting at her dining table, eating a sandwich and sipping on some coffee. The school in which she studied, Shivaji School of Excellence, had officially declared the beginning of summer vacations the day before. Her parents had gone to London because of some urgent work and were not to return for the next two weeks. Having finished her breakfast, she was just thinking of going for a bath when her phone issued a sound. She took it out from her pocket to see a message from Kamya, her best friend.

She had two best friends, Kamya and Shruti. While Kamya was more of an athletic person, Shruti loved science experiments. As Kanchi was a bit of both, they were reasonably well matched. As she opened the text, she realised that it had been copied from a school pamphlet. It read -

Trip to Khandala, Maharashtra. The school is proposing to send all the students aged above eleven to Khandala for an adventurous trip. The trip shall last for a week (23rd May–30th May). The school children shall leave the school at 9:00 AM. Information regarding the activities shall be given upon reaching Khandala. The students shall be made to stay at a resort. The expense of the entire trip shall be Rupees 9,450/- per student. The students are to get-

1. Two pairs of tracksuits
2. Two formal wear
3. Three casuals
4. Essential toiletries
5. Personal expenses (If any)

The payments must be made by 20 May. Late fees shall not be accepted.

Enjoy your Summer Vacation!

Shivaji School of Excellency

Beside that, Kamya had texted in her own words-

'Coming? If you convince your parents, I shall convince Shruti by saying that Khandala has got forests which are full of extraordinary researches. Please convince them, because I really want to go there and I shall not without my BFFs. Let's meet at Starbucks to discuss. Reply.'

Without hesitation, Kanchi texted back, 'Okay. Let's meet at twelve.' Quickly taking out a frock from her wardrobe, she drifted off to take a bath.

While she sat waiting for Kamya, and possibly Shruti too, she received a text from her mum. It was very short and said, 'Your dad saw a message regarding a trip. Do you want to go?' Kanchi hurriedly texted back, 'Yup. Kamya's parents have said okay, and if you agree, Shruti can come too.' Within minutes, her mom's reply came. It said, 'You father and I think that you should go, since you might get bored without us there anyway. As for the expenses, I shall talk to Shruti's mom and deposit the money in her account so that she can take it out and give it to you. What are you doing right now anyway?'

Pleasurably flushed with happiness and excitement, she began typing back, 'A lot of thanks, hugs and kisses, mom and dad. I am at Starbucks anyway, because Kamya wanted me to convince you both in front of her, but it is done now. Mum, can you give me some money for personal expenses?' Her mum's reply came, 'Alright, darling. There are four thousand rupees in the drawer of my wardrobe. You can take it. Okay, bye. I have to take a bath now. Love.'

Kanchi was just typing back a 'bye' when Kamya came in, looking jubilant and triumphant, followed by Shruti, looking equally happy. 'I have got a good news,' said Kanchi and Kamya in unison. 'What is it?' asked Kanchi and Shruti together.

'Fine. I will tell you first. I went to Shruti's place and managed to convince Shruti's parents to send Shruti to our Khandala school trip. Now, since both of us are going, there is a pretty good chance that your parents will be convinced easily too. What do you say? Should I speak to them on your phone or will you?' asked Kamya gleefully.

'That is awesome. It is even more awesome because I managed to convince my parents through texts. I was chatting with mum while waiting for you both. Why are you late, anyway?' asked Kanchi, smiling genuinely.

'That is great. We will have lots of fun in Khandala,' shouted Kamya, overexcited with happiness.

'Let's eat some snacks. All this anxiety and anticipation has been killing me,' said Shruti. While being the scientist of their group, she was also a great foodie. Kanchi and Kamya knew that their friend was an ecstatic bottomless pit when it came to food.

'Alright, let's take a quick snack. After that, we will head to my house to plan loads of things,' said Kanchi.

'I think we should first go and submit the fees. That is the prime responsibility,' said Kamya thoughtfully.

'Yeah, but what are you going to do about the fees, Kanchi?' asked Shruti.

'Mum is going to talk to one of yours mum. She must have already. She is going to send the money to the account of whomever she talks to,' Kanchi said. She refrained from using Shruti's name because Kamya used to get upset easily. Though she did not want to say it, Kanchi knew that Shruti was much more responsible and Kanchi's mom trusted her parents more then Kamya's.

'Okay, then. To know whose mom Kanchi's mum has connected to, let us call them and enquire. Let us call my mum first,' said Kamya matter-of-factly, bringing Kanchi back to her senses.

'Okay,' agreed Shruti. Kanchi didn't say anything, but nodded to show her agreement.

Kamya dialled her mum's number. Obviously, she said that she had not received any call from Kanchi's mother and that no one had deposited any money in her account. When they dialled Shruti's mum's number, she told them that she had received the money and that they could collect it by going to Shruti's house.

After collecting the money, they went to their school to deposit the fee at the reception. After that, Kamya went to her house to have lunch, while Shruti escorted Kanchi to her house so that she could have lunch there too. Since her parents were not there, she used to eat her lunch at the school canteen. During the holidays, however, she had to have lunch at one of her friends' place.

The trio couldn't count how the days flew before the trip. During the trip, they had the time of their lives. They enjoyed the beauty of Khandala and each other's company. After all, they were BFFs!

Will and Won't

Nishtha Trivedi was a beautiful and bold girl studying in New Delhi. She had a straight nose with beautiful round blue eyes. Her deep red lips concealed her very white teeth. She had waist length silvery straight hair. She was tall and had a slender neck. Though she lived in India, she was born in Paris and had stayed there for two years. Her father was Indian, but her mother was French. Like her daughter, she too had deep blue eyes, along with waist length silvery hair. But Nishtha had inherited her father's straight nose.

One lazy Sunday morning, Nishtha's mother called out, 'Nitu (Nishtha's pet name), come down quickly! Your father has an urgent call from his office. He has to go to France for a business tour immediately. I haven't seen my parents for a while now too, so I have decided to go with him. Come down and give your reply, quickly, because his office colleagues are asking how many tickets are to be booked.'

'Coming, maman (mum in French)!' Nishtha shouted back, descending the stairs. 'I don't want to go. My exams are coming and if I don't score above 95% this semester, I won't be able to win the Academically Excellent prize. And I certainly won't be able to score that much if I miss exams,' said Nishtha as soon as she reached downstairs.

'Whom are you fooling, Nitu? I know that your exams don't start for the next two months,' said her mother in a stern voice.

'Oh. Okay. Alright. Well we–I mean, Eklavya, Beth and I, want to enjoy together. I mean, Beth's father has got us tickets to attend the World Film Festival that is happening in Delhi. So, I thought that I would invite Beth and Eklavya over to our place and we will have a sleepover here and then go to the film festival together,' said Nishtha sheepishly. Eklavya and Beth were Nishtha's best friends. They were unique because they were very different from each other. Beth, or Bertha Amelia, was from London. She was blonde and had curly golden hair. Meanwhile, Eklavya or Eklavyini Konkan was a native south Indian. She was dark and had long jet black hair.

'What do this Eklavya's parents do?' asked Nishtha's mom.

'I think her father is a taxi driver and her mum is a housewife,' replied Nishtha simply.

'You couldn't find anyone else to be friends with than this Eklavya?' said Nishtha's mum pointedly.

Nishtha was shocked. She didn't understand what her mum had said. How could anyone judge or decide another person's character or personality by asking what his or her father did?

'Mum, once you meet Eklavya, you will eat your own words. She is really nice. She is so patient and kind. Anyway, I am not going to France,' said Nishtha in a hurt voice.

'Akshay! Tell your colleagues to book two tickets,' shouted Nishtha's mum to her dad, Akshay, who was sitting in another room.

'Okay, Isa darling,' came back Akshay's reply.

'Can I go and take a bath now, maman?' asked Nishtha, who was still in her night gown. When Isabelle nodded, she ran upstairs. Closing her bed room door behind her, she gazed around her room. She would be free, she thought, free for a few days where no one would decide her wills and won'ts for her. Humming a happy tune, she went to bathe.

'Mum, I am going to Eklavya's. Together, we will round up Beth and eat ice cream,' shouted Nishtha half an hour later, slipping on her slippers.

'Wait. Go to Beth's place and round her up first. Tell her to go and get Eklavya then. You will not go to that girl's house,' said her mum in a commanding voice.

'But mum-'

'Do so, or go back to your room.'

'But-'

'Go back to your room, Nishtha.'

'Alright.'

Marching out in the brilliant sun, Nishtha was swearing under her breath, 'What does she think...'

Reaching Beth's house after a good ten minutes of walk, she ringed the doorbell. A lady opened the door and smiled upon seeing Nishtha. 'Nishtha dear, I am so sorry, but Bertha can't come to play with you today. We are packing because we are leaving for a two weeks' trip to Las Vegas. It was decided this morning only. Our flight is booked for tomorrow morning,' the lady, Beth's mum, Andromeda said.

'Oh. Does that mean that Beth won't be able to join Eklavya and me for the World Film Festival?' asked Nishtha, trying to keep her voice casual and not too crestfallen and dejected.

'No, no. Bertha's father was not able to get the tickets. So to cheer Bertha up, her father and I decided to take this trip. I was about to call you and Eklavya too. I am so sorry,' said Andromeda apologetically.

'It's okay, aunty. Can I come in and help you with the packing?' asked Nishtha.

'Thank you for asking, dear. Come in,' said Andromeda, looking pleased.

Nishtha spent the next half an hour helping Andromeda and Beth with their packing. Biding them farewell then, Nishtha trotted back home. When she reached back home, she found her mother sitting on the sofa, waiting for her.

'What flavour did you have, Nishtha?' asked her mom as soon as she saw Nishtha entering.

'No, maman. I didn't eat ice cream. When I turned up at Beth's place, her mum told me that Beth's father had not been able to get the tickets. So, to cheer her up, aunty and uncle decided to take her on a trip to Las Vegas. When I reached their place, they were packing for it. I decided to stay back and help them, since their flight is tomorrow morning itself,' replied Nishtha, feeling proud, that she had helped someone.

Instead, her mum stood up and shouted, 'Nishtha! You should have come straight back home. You are not their servant that you help them with their packing. Today, they made you do slavery. Tomorrow, they will tell you to clean their house, will you do so in the name of help too?' Isa sat down fuming.

'Maman! How could you? You are behaving as though you are a supremacist. You are discriminating. They are my friends and for your information, Andromeda aunty didn't ask me to help her with the packing. I offered to do it myself. I can't shut myself off from people because of their economic background. I am not like you,' shouted Nishtha, now on the verge of tears.

'How dare you, Nishtha? I firmly believe that people should stay in the place they deserve. I am proud of my riches and grand glamour,' shouted her mum.

'SHAME ON YOU, MAMAN!' bellowed Nishtha and before Isa could stop her, she had stormed away to her room. Nishtha entered her bedroom and closed the door behind her with a loud thud. She lay down on her bed, tears pouring from her eyes. Her mum's words nested in her brain like a disease. Crying her heart out, she did not come to know when she fell asleep.

Two hours later, Nishtha woke up with a start. Someone was banging at her bedroom door. She got up and opened the door to find her mother standing in the doorway, a lunch tray in her hand. She entered the room and kept the tray on the table. She then sat down on Nishtha's bed and said, 'I am so sorry. I shouldn't have said all those things. After you came to your room, I realized my fault. You were right after all, a person is rich or poor from one's thoughts and heart. I have always imposed my thoughts and beliefs on you. I also shouted at you. Forgive me, Nishtha.'

Nishtha smiled. Her mom had finally understood. She jerked her head to one side, which meant, *forget it*. Perhaps her mum understood it because she hugged her a moment later, and whispered in her ear, 'Thank you.'

Minku Realises His Mistake

Once upon a time, there lived a witty crow, named Minku. He was very lazy and always fooled the other animals due to his witty nature and their kind and innocent nature. A kind mole, named Chinu, lived in the same jungle as Minku. One day, Minku thought of a plan in order to fool Chinu. He went to Chinu's house and told him, Hi, Chinu! I have a very bad headache, but I have to clean my house. Will you please help me with the cleaning? It would be really nice of you."

'Of course. I will be happy to do that,' said Chinu.

Both of them went to Minku's nest then and Chinu started cleaning the nest. After a while, Chinu grew a little apprehensive that why was he the only one cleaning the house, while Minku was not helping even a bit. Still, he continued the job, thinking that it would be rude on his part to ask Minku why he was not helping, especially since Minku had a severe headache. Chinu spent the next two hours thinking this, till he became very tired.

"Minku! I have been cleaning your house tirelessly for hours, but you didn't even offer to help or ask me to take rest for a while,' Chinu complained. Minku replied, 'I am so sorry, Chinu.

As you are aware, I have a severe headache, so I was taking some rest and could not help you out.'

"Okay, Minku. Now that I have cleaned up the house, I will go home,' said Chinu.

But the lazy and selfish Minku was not satisfied with the cleaning that Chinu had done for him and wanted to extract more work out of Chinu. 'My dear Chinu, thank you very much for neatly cleaning the house, but you know, I am still not feeling well and some of my friends are coming home for dinner. Do you mind helping me cook as well?'

Chinu started doubting Minku's intentions, however, he thought that leaving Minku like that would not be proper on his behalf either.

'Okay, Minku. I can stay for some more time, but not till dinner,' replied Chinu in a very polite manner. Minku was overjoyed that he could make a fool out of Chinu and make him cook as well. Minku was very proud of his crooked skill.

As Chinu started cooking, Minku lazed around and increased the number of dishes for Chinu to cook. Chinu, being a very helpful and kind hearted friend, did whatever Minku asked him to do. After a few hours when the work was done, Chinu wished Minku a pleasant evening with his friends and walked back to his home.

While walking back, Chinu met his friend Rocku, the raccoon. 'Hi, dear Chinu! How are you doing?' Rocku asked.

Chinu replied in a very dull and low voice, 'Uffff, I am so damn tired.'

'Why? What happened, dear?' asked Rocku.

'Don't ask me how Minku played mischief with me today and made me do his daily chores. He cheated me and lied to me.' That's how Chinu narrated all that Minku had done with him.

Rocku showed true concern for his friend and replied, 'Oh, I am so sorry to know all this. Are you not aware of his dirty habits? He has already done this before with all our animal friends, including me.'

Then, both of them decided to expose Minku and teach him a lesson.

After a few days, both of them made a plan and went to Minku's house, offering to clean up his house and cook food for him. Minku thought it to be a great opportunity to exploit them and make use of their kindness. He said, 'You two are such loving and caring friends. I was just remembering you as I am not well today.'

When Chinu started doing his work, Rocku started recording everything on his camera. During that time, Minku was thoroughly enjoying his day by gossiping with his other friends over the phone, singing, listening to songs and dancing as well. There was no sign of illness in any of his activities. Those things were also captured by Rocku. When all the work was complete, both of them went away quietly and proceeded straight to Sherru, the King of the jungle.

'Your Highness! We have come to you with a complaint against Minku. He has cheated us and our friends by telling lies and exploiting us. Today, we have got proof of his deeds too. May we show it to you?' requested Chinu and Rocku.

Sherru was kind enough to watch the video and believed them, as he had already heard of Minku's mischiefs form the other animals as well. He made up his mind and said, 'Enough is enough. I will punish that stupid Minku and make him apologise to all the animals. I will also ensure that nobody goes to him, even in the case of a true emergency.'

The very next day, Sherru called for a general

body meeting of all the animals and exposed Minku's deeds in a very humiliating manner, and declared the above mentioned punishments for him.

Minku was shocked by this and apologized to all the members. Thereafter, he changed his attitude and the other animals became friends with him gradually, and they all lived happily ever after.

Kindness Revealed

Once upon a time, there lived three sisters. The eldest one–Gabrielle, was a very greedy and lazy girl. She was also very ugly, but she boasted that she was the prettiest of all. The second one–Isabelle, was not that greedy, but not too philanthropic either. She was a fair girl. The youngest one–Clarabelle, was the prettiest and the most selfless girl of all.

Once, their mother sent Clarabelle to the old sage Mount's house in the deep dark woods with some apple tarts, veg burgers and a green apple. By the time Clarabelle reached the sage's house, it was already dark. She gave the old sage her dinner and slept on the floor, giving him the bed. The next morning, the sage gave her a big bag of gold coins for her kind and selfless nature. Clarabelle went home happily.

When Isabelle heard about the fortune of her younger sister, she decided to go to the old sage's house too. Taking some porridge, sandwiches and apple juice, she set out to Sage Mount's house. Just like her younger sister, when she reached the old sage's house, it had gotten dark. She stayed at the sage's house for the night too. She gave him only a little portion of her food and made him sleep on the floor. The next morning, she got a small bag of gold coins from the sage. She returned home not that happily, but not too sad as well. When Isabelle and Clarabelle were telling their mother about the fortune that they had received from old sage Mount, greedy Gabrielle heard them and decided to go to the sage's house too with her best friends–Fleur and Matilda.

The next morning, the three girls set out to the sage's house with roasted chicken fries and vegetarian pizzas. When the three of them reached the sage's house, it was already dark and they decided to stay at the sage's house for the night. They did not give the sage anything from their food. Instead, they made him walk a few kilometers to go to the well and get water for them, as they had forgotten to get water from their homes and the roasted chicken was really spicy. At night, Gabrielle made her best friends and the old sage sleep outside in the shivering cold, while she enjoyed the comfort and warmth of the room by herself. The next day, the old sage gave Gabrielle a punishment which tormented her life and made her a maniac for a period of time.

He dramatically cut off a chunk of hair from the right side of her head, which was a matter of great shame for girls in those times. She begged for mercy at his feet, but he did not pay any heed to the oaths and promises that she made of becoming a kind, selfless and philanthropic girl. She went home crying and all the way back, her mind was occupied only by the fear of her mother's reaction and the teasing of her sisters–Clarabelle and Isabelle.

When she reached home, her mother was in the kitchen. She rushed towards her and hugged her tightly. 'What happened?' she asked, but suddenly understood everything upon seeing the missing chunk of hair on her daughter's head.

CRASHHH!!! The bowl carrying the Zucchini salad slipped out of her hands. Clara and Isa came down running and entered the kitchen, their faces aghast. They too saw the missing chunk of hair on their sister's head and understood everything, just like their mother. They hugged their sister and the four of them quickly resolved that only Gabrielle could set things right again, if she would go back and heartily apologise to the old sage.

All of them went to the sage. Though Gabrielle hesitated a little at first, she geared up her confidence after talking to the sage for a few minutes. The old sage was indeed touched by the kind words of Gabrielle and decided to forgive her by using his magic to regrow her hair. Soon after growing her hair back, the sage bid Gabrielle farewell and promised her that he would keep on meeting her in the future. The family, now full of happiness and kindness, returned back.

Shardha Regrets Bullying

Shardha was a spoiled brat. She was always pampered by her parents. They fulfilled her every wish, be it reasonable or not. That's why, Shardha never learnt to value the things that were given to her. She studied in Barcelones School in Mumbai. She was tall and slender, with jet black hair that were mostly tied in a long plait. She had almond shaped eyes and pink lips. She was a very beautiful thirteen year old. She had two friends (rather, servants), Niharika Subramanian and Anoushka Bharadwaj. They both did whatever Shardha did. Other than this, Shardha was also awfully short tempered.

One day, as soon as Shardha, Niharika and Anoushka reached school, they saw a crowd of people admiring and interacting with someone. Since people were standing too close to each other, they could not see to whom they were all talking. Shardha gave Niharika and Anoushka an ordering look, and they obliged at once by pushing people away to make way for Shardha. They shouted, 'Make way. The elegant beauty of Mumbai, Shardha Sharma, is coming. Get out!' they added to a terrified looking girl, who jumped and ran towards the main school building, staggering as she went.

Smirking satisfactorily, Anoushka and Niharika turned in hope to find Shardha pleased, but she just shrugged and started moving. Anoushka and Niharika, looking slightly crestfallen, followed her. This was another problem with Shardha. She never appreciated another's work. When she moved to the front, she saw a girl there with rosy red lips, beautiful and exuberant eyes, wavy brown hair that reached down to her waist and pretty snowy cheeks. She was tall and slender, with a dazzling smile on her lips. She looked so simple, yet breathtaking. Even Niharika and Anoushka gaped at her, their eyes wide with surprise. Shardha was the only one in the crowd who gaped at her with anger and shock, and not surprise. Little did she know that this girl was indeed more pretty than her.

'Hi, my name is Angelina, Angelina Madison. I am a newcomer to this school and want to make a lot of charming friends. You seem to be smart. Can we be friends?' asked Angelina in a soft voice, extending a hand of friendship. Shardha was about to shake it off rather rudely, when a brilliant idea came to her mind. If she became Angelina's best friend, then no matter how many rumours she leaked about her, Angelina would never suspect her. She looked so innocent by heart.

'Yeah, of course. You are a newcomer at Barcelones School and as a student here, it is my duty to make you feel comfortable. We can be best friends. These are my friends, Niharika Subramanian and Anoushka Bhardawaj,' replied Shardha in a falsely sweet voice.

'That is very good. Thank you so much. If you could escort me to class eighth A,' said Angelina, overjoyed.

'Yeah, Angelina. Follow me, Niharika and Anoushka.'

Within a few weeks, Shardha had managed to win Angelina's trust completely by helping her out in learning and adjusting to the new environment of their school. One evening, while eating crisps at Shardha's house, Niharika asked Shardha, 'Shardha, why did you befriend that scum Angelina? Everyone saw your look of disgust when you first saw her. Is it a part of your mastermind plan, huh?'

'Yup, my dear. I am going to leak some rumours about her and start whispers about her. Since I am now labelled as her true best friend, she would not suspect me either. I will make her life miserable,' shot back Shardha, smirking.

'But why are you doing all this in the first place? She has not humiliated or insulted you publicly,' asked Anoushka.

'It's just the fact that she exists,' replied Shardha scornfully. 'Shardha, can we go to the library together? Shardha, can I borrow your pen? Please, Shardha?' she added, mimicking Angelina.

'But when are we going to execute the actual plan?' Anoushka asked Shardha.

'Tomorrow, the results of the periodic tests are going to be declared. If that Angelina does well, I am going to leak the rumour that she did so by cheating. If she doesn't, I will invent a few insulting nicknames based on her percentage and spread them. Isn't that a mastermind plan?' replied Shardha.

'Aren't you worried about the results, Shardha? I have done fairly well in Chemistry, solved eighteen questions from twenty, knew five answers without any doubt, while the rest are the ones with some doubt or guesswork. English is going to be alright. I am worried about Mythology, Mathematics and Mythology. Civics must be fine,' piped up Niharika, looking anxious.

Shardha replied unconcerned, 'I am not worried because if I score badly, which I will, I will just put the blame on my tutor, which I always do. My parents will believe me, as usual. Okay, bye now. I have to get my nails trimmed. My nail art is wearing off.' Anoushka and Niharika recognized their dismissal and got up to leave.

The next morning at school, their class teacher came in with a paper that recorded everyone's percentage. The class teacher started, 'I must tell you, class, that the results are less than satisfactory. I am going to personally call the parents of those who have scored less then 45%. So, let us start. Kavya Bansal, 64%. Angelina Madison...' The class teacher stopped at Angelina's name. His face grew so pale that he seemed as if he would faint. He continued, 'Miss Madison, you are this session's topper. You have scored 98.9%. Please come here and make the acknowledgements.'

Angelina clapped her hands to her mouth. Beaming positively, she made her way to the teacher's desk. She started in a voice overwhelmed with sincerity, 'I thank you, sir, firstly for giving me the stage to express my heartfelt gratitude to some people, and secondly, for giving me all the knowledge which was needed to acquire this milestone. I will take this moment to thank my parents who were and are always a source of inspirational and never ending encouragement for me. But most of all, I would like to thank someone who brings immense comfort to me. That person is Shardha Sharma.'

Shardha was surprised to hear her own name. Before she could understand, Angelina had moved on. 'A friend is a person who laughs with you in your joyful situations, and cries with you in a sorrowful situation, but Shardha is a person who did not let any sorrowful situations come near me, while crying is far away. I thank you, Shardha, for making my life beautiful in this new place. That's all, sir.' With that, she came back to her seat.

There were tears in Shardha's eyes, tears of shame and guilt. How could she have ever thought of discrediting Angelina Madison? She decided that very moment that she would reveal everything about her conspiracy to Angelina. Meanwhile, the class teacher resumed, 'Oh, is this about Shardha Sharma? Okay then, let me tell her percentage as well, 62%. Niharika Subramanian, 48% and Anoushka Bharadwaj, 73%. The rest will be given after the recess.' He got up from his seat then and left.

Dodging everyone, Shardha went over to Angelina's desk and blurted out the truth about the whole conspiracy to her. After she had finished, Angelina said, 'Okay. I forgive you even before you apologise, because you realised your mistake before I made you. You could have done all those bad things with me, but you didn't. So, now we are friends without any guilt, right?'

Shardha grabbed the hand that she had extended, bringing about an awesome end to an emotional story.

Thank You

My Dear Reader,

My sincere and heartfelt gratitude goes out to you for having chosen and read my FIRST piece of writing in the form of this book. I hope you enjoyed my style of fiction writing.

Your reviews, opinions and feedback matter to me a lot.

I can be reached @ anantineemishra07@gmail.com

Instagram: anantineejhumpamishra

Love you all…

A